TIME FLYERS

COOKiNG
UP TROUBLE

COOKiNG UP TROUBLE

BY PERDITA FINN

SCHOLASTIC INC.

New York   Toronto   London   Auckland   Sydney
Mexico City   New Delhi   Hong Kong   Buenos Aires

ISBN 0-439-74435-0

12 11 10 9 8 7 6 5 4 3 2 1   6 7 8 9 10 11/0

Printed in the U.S.A.
First printing, November 2006

For Donna Albright,

a teacher who makes history come alive

1 RECIPE FOR DISASTER

Josh and his best friend, Neil Carmody, were playing War on the long bus ride home when they heard the sonic boom.

"What was that?" exclaimed Neil, dropping his deck.

"Some kind of high-powered jet," answered Josh, lying.

While Neil was picking up his scattered cards, Josh looked over at his sister, Katie, in the seat across the aisle. He'd heard that sound before. He knew it wasn't a jet. Did she have the same thought he did?

His eyes met hers and she nodded. She'd heard it, too. Plus, outside the bus window, she had seen a brilliant blue light flash across the gray November sky. It could only mean one thing.

Another one had just arrived.

"So I'm coming over today so we can finally finish the game. Right, Josh? Right?" Neil said, trying to get his attention.

"No!" Katie jumped in. "You can't."

"No," added Josh. "I don't think so."

"What? You let your little sister order you around?"

"Be quiet, Neil." Josh glared at him. "Katie's right. You can't come over. I forgot we're having special guests today."

Katie nodded her head urgently. "Here's our stop, Josh." She grabbed her brother by the arm. "'Bye, Neil!"

Both kids raced off the bus and up the road toward home, their heavy book bags slapping against their backs. It was a cold afternoon and their breath came out in short, smoky puffs as they ran.

"If we hurry, maybe we can get there before he does," said Katie.

"I hope this one doesn't arrive naked," added Josh.

Their mother was folding laundry in the living room when they burst in the front door. "Close the door," she said. "It's freezing out. I'm sure it's going to start snowing any day now, and it's not even Thanksgiving."

"Has he come yet?" asked Katie breathlessly.

"Where is he?" demanded Josh. "What's he look like? Has he got clothes on?"

"Whatever are the two of you talking about?" asked their mother. "And would you please hang up your coats? I'm not the maid around here."

"Mom!" shouted Katie. "The Time Flyer! Where's the new kid from Time Flyers?"

Time Flyers was the student exchange program Mrs. Lexington had signed up with at the beginning of the year. Every month, a new kid from a foreign country would arrive to stay with the Lexingtons for a brief visit. The only problem was that these kids *also* came from back in time — and Josh and Katie had to keep that fact a secret from everybody, especially their parents.

Mrs. Lexington stood up, a large pile of freshly washed towels in her arms. "I'm sorry, kids. Didn't I tell you? I wrote Mr. Dee, the director of the program, and told him I thought we'd take a break over the holiday. Let us catch our breath and all."

"That's fine by me!" said Josh, heading into the kitchen to get a bite to eat. He was completely relieved not to have to explain to some ancient Egyptian kid why he had to wear pants to school.

But Katie just stood there. Something wasn't right.

"Grab those sheets, will you, sweetie?" asked her mother. "I could really use a little help putting things away."

Katie hesitated. "Mom?"

"Yes, dear?"

"Are there any other families in town that host Time Flyer exchange students?"

"I don't think so. You know, it's a very hard program to get into. They only take a few families each year. We're awfully lucky."

"Yeah," agreed Katie, absentmindedly. "Mom, I have to check something." She ran out of the room, forgetting all about neatly folded sheets.

"Oh, for goodness sake," muttered Mrs. Lexington. "You'd think somebody would give me a hand around here sometimes."

Josh was in the kitchen waiting for a frozen pizza to heat up in the toaster oven when Katie rushed in.

"C'mon." She grabbed him by the arm. "We've got to talk. Something's wrong."

"You're right, toad-face. My pizza's burning. Let me go, will ya?"

Katie shook her head at her brother. "I can't believe you. Aren't you the least bit curious about what happened to the Time Flyer?"

"You heard Mom. We're not getting one this time."

"But the sonic boom. The blue light. Those are the signs every time. A kid from Time Flyers *always* arrives after them." Katie pulled on Josh's arm.

"Let go, will ya? Maybe one will show up later on and then we can spend the next month freaked out about all the weird things he's doing. But for now, I'm sitting down on the couch to eat my pizza *in peace*."

"No, you're not. You're coming with me." Even though Katie was several inches shorter than her brother, she was surprisingly strong. She also pinched hard and usually got away with it because she was the youngest. After a short scuffle, she managed to drag her brother outside.

"We've got to assume that a Time Flyer arrived," she explained. "But where is he? The last thing we want is some out-of-time weirdo challenging someone in town to a duel."

"Or going to the bathroom in someone's soccer trophy," muttered Josh, thinking of Jack, their earlier Time Flyer from Elizabethan England.

"Do you remember where the bus was when we heard the sonic boom?"

"Yeah, right after Evergreen Lane. I'd just taken one of Neil's queens with an ace."

"Okay, then, that's where we're headed."

"But that's over a mile away!" said Josh, thinking of his pizza.

"Walk fast," said Katie.

As they hurried down the street, they looked around for kids who didn't belong. But Katie knew the real problem was that they didn't know what to expect this time. Would it be a caveman in a fur-covered cape or a Viking boy in a horned hat? Would they even be able to recognize their visitor? Katie wasn't so sure. Her mind raced with possibilities. But all she actually saw were kids riding their bikes, people raking up leaves in their yards, and a couple of joggers.

When she saw their neighbor Mrs. Eldridge walking her three dogs, Katie stopped to talk to her. "We're looking for a friend of ours, Mrs. Eldridge. You haven't seen anyone around who looks a little lost, have you?"

"Lost? Lost? You know, I think *I* might be a bit lost. Which direction was I going in when you stopped me?"

"You were coming from Evergreen, Mrs. Eldridge," said Josh.

"Ah, good. Then it's time for dinner. C'mon, babies." She headed up the street with her dogs.

Josh gave Katie a look of total exasperation. "Are you satisfied now? No Time Flyer anywhere. You owe me big."

"I guess you're right." Katie sighed. "Let's take the shortcut back home."

The shortcut was a worn deer path through the woods behind the houses. The trees were almost bare now, and Josh and Katie's feet crunched over dry, brown oak leaves as they walked. Josh kept muttering about how hungry he was and how Katie had ruined yet another afternoon. "And I didn't even get to hang out with Neil because of you," he complained.

But as they came around an old rotten tree, Katie suddenly stopped. "*Shh*," she said. "Did you hear that?"

"What?"

"That noise. It sounds like someone's crying."

"Ah, it's just a bird or something. Let's get going."

And then they saw her.

Just ahead of them on the path was a girl. And both Josh and Katie knew, without even talking to her, that there was *no way* she was from their century.

2 THE MISSING INGREDIENT

She was dressed in long wool skirts and a white kerchief with a red cape pulled around her, and was leaning against a tree, clearly exhausted. Her face was smudged with tears, but the moment she saw Josh and Katie coming toward her, she wiped the tears from her face and backed away.

"Begone, savages!" she yelled. She picked up a stick and hurled it toward Josh and Katie. She had good aim. Katie managed to duck just in time.

"It's all right," said Katie. "We're friends."

"Yeah!" said Josh. "Settle down. We're the rescue squad."

But the girl didn't listen. "Away from me! Away from me!" she shouted. In her panic, she tripped over her long skirts and fell. Immediately, she was up again with a rock in her hand. She threw it so hard, it knocked a piece of bark off a tree next to Katie's ear.

"Will you take a chill pill?" said Katie as the girl picked up a big branch and held it in front of her like a spear.

"Whoa!" said Josh. "Put that thing down. We know you're a Time Flyer. It's no problem."

"A Time Flyer?" repeated the girl warily, the branch still in her hand. "Nay! I am a Separatist from Leiden."

"You don't have to keep it a secret from us," said Josh, approaching her slowly. "We know all about Master Dee and how you came into the future using his computer."

"And we promise to keep it a secret," added Katie. She gave the girl a reassuring smile.

"Thou speak English well," was all the girl answered. She seemed surprised.

"Right," said Josh. "That's what we speak in America in the twenty-first century."

"Are ye Wampanoags or Narragansett?" She started to back away again, looking wild.

"What?" said Josh. "Neither. I told you, we're Americans."

"Wait a minute," said Katie. "Those are Native American tribes. Do you think we're *Native* Americans?"

"I know not what ye be nor how thee came to speak the tongue of England." She paused, considering. "But if ye have met men of God and know something of our ways, then perhaps you boys can guide me back to my village."

"Boys?" said Katie. She looked like she really had been hit by a rock. "What makes you think I'm a boy? I'm a girl."

"You gotta admit, Katie. It's a mistake anyone could make." Josh laughed while Katie glared at him.

"But your hair, your breeches," persisted the strange girl. "What savage people are ye whose women dress like men?"

"You poor kid." Josh looked at her sympathetically. After all, if he'd just found himself lost in the woods in a strange country and in a completely different time, he'd be freaked out, too. "My name's Josh Lexington," he began, speaking calmly and quietly. "And this is my sister, Katie. She's a girl, although I agree with you, it's hard to tell sometimes."

"Thanks," Katie muttered, wishing she had a stick in *her* hand.

The girl looked them over carefully. "Mayhap I must trust thee," she said. "Night comes and 'tis the truth, I am lost in these dark woods."

"What's your name?" asked Josh.

"I be Humility Cooper, late of Leiden, Holland, and now of Plymouth Colony."

"Wow!" said Josh.

"You're a Pilgrim?" asked Katie. "A real Pilgrim?"

"Nay," said Humility. "I make no pilgrimage. I but took chase after a Wampanoag boy that had stolen an hourglass."

"What?" said Katie interrupting her. "Someone stole your hourglass?" Every Time Flyer carried a golden hourglass that transported them from one century to another.

"Nay, not mine," continued the girl. "But I was sure he had taken it from one of our families. I knew he was a thief when he ran. But when I caught him and lay my hands on the timepiece, all became darkness except for blue lightning and a sound that shuddered in my ears. When I opened my eyes, I found myself here."

"Wait a minute," said Katie. "I think I'm getting it. Do you know Master Dee?"

"Nay, I know not this gentleman," said the girl.

"Were you planning on being an exchange student?" asked Josh.

The girl shook her head, confused.

"You don't know what Time Flyers is, do you?" asked Katie.

The girl shook her head again.

"Oh, boy," said Josh.

"Oh, boy," said Katie.

What they both knew at that moment was that Humility Cooper was an accident. Probably some Native American boy was supposed to be off on his own time-travel adventure right now. Only he wasn't, and Humility Cooper was.

"You shouldn't take other people's stuff," said Katie.

"Ye say this to *me*? 'Twas *I* that was protecting our colony from a thief."

"That is such a stereotype," said Katie. "Just because he's different from you doesn't mean he's a thief." She knew Humility probably didn't know any better, but this was beginning to irritate her.

"Your tribe may inflict upon me all manner of punishments, but I will return nothing until we speak of this matter with the elders of our colony," announced Humility.

"Okay," announced Josh. "We're going to have to get a few things straight — and fast. Humility,

15

we're not Indians. You're not in Plymouth anymore or anywhere near it. In fact, you're not even in the . . . when were the Pilgrims, anyway, Katie?"

"Sixteen hundred something, I think."

"Right," said Josh. "Humility, I don't know how to tell this to you any other way, but you're almost four hundred years in the future."

Humility put her hands over her eyes and shrieked. "Witches, begone from me! Away, away with you!"

Katie looked at Josh, throwing up her hands helplessly. "We can't bring her home like this to Mom and Dad," she whispered. "The other ones were hard enough. And they were prepared to be in the future!"

"But it's getting dark," Josh said. Already it was hard to see the path, and he knew their mother would be getting worried. He took a deep breath. "Humility. We're pretty nice people. . . ."

"Begone! I will hear nothing more of your strange lunacies!" In an instant she'd bent down and grabbed another handful of rocks to throw.

"Lunacies?" repeated Katie. "*We're* not the

16

ones throwing rocks." She slowly walked over to Humility. "Drop the weapons, all right?" After a few moments of hesitation Humility let the rocks slip out of her hand. Josh was impressed. His little sister's toughness never ceased to amaze him.

"Look," continued Katie. "I can't even imagine how scary and weird this must be." Josh nodded his head in agreement. "But please listen and try and understand, okay? First of all, I'm not a boy, and we're not witches. But you are in a mess of trouble. And there are only two people in this world who can get you out of it. Me and my brother. So would you please come with us?"

Humility looked at Katie warily. "I warn thee. Captain Standish is a fierce guard and if thou hurt me, he and his men will come after thee."

"Captain Standish? You mean *Miles* Standish?" asked Josh.

"Aye," said Humility, surprised. "Do you know him?"

"Kind of. I mean, I played him in the second-grade Thanksgiving play. Wasn't he friends with that Priscilla gal?"

"Aye," said Humility. "Captain Standish does like Mistress Mullins, but so does John Alden."

"Oh, yeah," Josh said, remembering. "But he won't do anything about it. Isn't that right?"

"'Tis right," said Humility. Her whole face brightened and she gave Josh the briefest of smiles. "When didst thou visit our colony? I remember thee not."

"Well, I've never actually been there. But I'd love to hear about it. Why don't you tell me while we head on home?"

Humility nodded her head and then began walking and talking excitedly with Josh about all the different people she knew. "Governor Bradford is, of course, a fine man. . . ."

Josh waved at Katie to follow them. Katie shook her head, surprised that Josh was able to actually have a conversation with a girl, especially one from a different century. She followed behind them, trying to catch everything Humility was saying.

They emerged from the woods just a few houses

down from the Lexingtons' split-level ranch. Humility gasped as she looked up and down the street. "Where are we?" She grabbed Josh's arm.

"We told you," said Katie with a big sigh. "You're in the twenty-first century."

Just at that moment a black SUV roared by, followed by a tiny, turquoise sports car. Humility screamed, an ear-piercing shriek that made Josh hold his ears.

"What behemoths are these? What strange and terrible monsters? Oh, please, I beg of ye. Take me home at once!"

"They're just cars," said Katie.

"They're like carriages without horses," explained Josh. "But they are big and loud."

"Thou speakest truth?"

"Truth about what?" asked Josh.

"Do ye speak the truth about where I be? Have I really flown across time with no ship and no transport? How could such a marvel be?"

"We don't really know the specifics," began Josh.

"But we do know," continued Katie, "that it all has to do with the hourglass you stole from that boy."

"I told you. I did not steal it. *He* did. Would any Wampanoag boy have such a thing as this?" She reached into a pouch around her waist and pulled out the small golden timepiece.

"Can I see it?" asked Josh. "You can tell how long you're going to be here by the sand. If it's flowing really fast, you'll be back in Plymouth in no time."

"Yeah," said Katie. "Our last visitor only stayed a week. And he was from ancient Egypt. Maybe you'll even be able to go home tonight, since you're here by accident and all."

Humility handed the hourglass to Josh, who held it up to get a good look at it. He shook it, and held it up again. "Huh, that's strange," he said. "What do you think?" He handed the hourglass to his sister.

Katie looked at it. She flipped it over and looked at it again. "The sand's not moving at all!" she exclaimed.

"I noticed," agreed Josh. "Does that mean she's here forever?"

"Oh, no!" said Katie.

"What? What?" Humility clutched Josh's arm. "Am I truly lost in the wilderness of time? What is it I have done to deserve this? Can it be because I was late to meeting on the Sabbath?"

"Maybe it was because you stole that boy's hourglass!" said Katie.

"Give it a rest, Katie. Will ya?" snapped Josh. He patted Humility's hand reassuringly. "We'll figure this out," Josh said to her. "Mom will dash off an e-mail to Mr. Dee when we get home and have everything straightened out by dinner. No big deal."

But that's not what Katie was thinking. She was pretty sure this was going to be a very big deal indeed.

3 HOT WATER

"There you are," said Mrs. Lexington as the kids trouped through the front door. "I was getting worried. Your father's made us a fire because it's gotten so chilly." Just then Mrs. Lexington noticed Humility. "Oh!" she exclaimed. "I didn't know you were having a friend over for dinner."

"This is Humility Cooper, Mom," said Josh as Humility looked around the living room, her eyes wide. "She's from Time Flyers." Humility quickly curtsied and bowed her head without saying a word.

"But we're not getting anyone from Time Flyers this month," said Mrs. Lexington.

"She's an accident, Mom," whispered Katie so Humility wouldn't hear. "A big accident."

"Yeah," said Josh. "It seems like there's been some kind of mix-up. Can we e-mail Mr. Dee or the Time Flyers program to figure out what's going on? I don't think Humility was expecting to come here, either."

"But, Goody Lexington, I promise to be no burden," said Humility. "I can cook and sew and spin. I can prepare thy gardens for the winter and carry water and dig thy privy hole if need be and slop thy pigs and . . ."

"That's so nice of you," Mrs. Lexington interrupted, "but we don't have any pigs, dear."

"*Sssh!*" whispered Katie to Humility.

"Who's this?" said their father, coming into the room from the kitchen. "I didn't know we had any Amish kids in the neighborhood."

"Abner, we have an unexpected Time Flyers exchange student," said Mrs. Lexington in a hushed voice.

"What?"

"This is Humility Cooper, Dad," said Josh, introducing her again. "She's from Holland, sort of, originally, I guess."

"Oh, I see. You're wearing your national dress," said Mr. Lexington cheerfully. "Have you got on the wooden shoes?"

Humility shook her head, confused. "It has been many months since we left Holland, but I need no new shoes, sir. And I can make clothes for you and your family if need be — mittens and new caps and scarves for the coming cold."

"That's awfully nice of you," said Mr. Lexington, and then turning to his wife he added in a hushed voice, "It really is something the way they just drop these kids off at all times of the night with no warning. . . ."

"I know, Abner. I know. But let's not have this conversation now." She raised her eyebrows at her husband, who nodded his head. They glanced toward Humility, who had bent low again in a curtsy.

"Humility, dear," said Mrs. Lexington. "Forgive me for not being more welcoming. We were just a little surprised, that's all. But we'll get this all straightened out and have a lovely visit together."

"I assure you, Goody Lexington, I eat very little," answered Humility in a low voice. "I will earn my keep. I can even snare rabbits and gut them and clean them myself. Of necessity I have lately learned to do so."

"Oh, my!" Mrs. Lexington turned slightly pale. "No, dear, I don't think that'll be necessary. I'm sure Abner's made enough lasagna for everyone. Now, where are you *supposed* to be?"

"'Tis in Plymouth that we now reside."

"Oh, I see. You were probably supposed to fly into Boston. I'll just dash off a quick e-mail to Mr. Dee. Kids, why don't you get Humility settled in upstairs? She can have your bed, Katie, and I'll bring the air mattress up for you later."

Great, thought Katie. She took Humility by the arm and led her upstairs. There was a lot they had to go over fast — toilets and electric lights and clothing and beds and who knew what else. Humility seemed dazed by it all. She stood in the bathroom, flushing the toilet over and over again, her eyes big with wonder. She clicked the lights on and off, on and off, on and off, until Katie stopped her. "Let's save some electricity, all right?"

"How many families sleep here?" Humility asked when Katie brought her into her room.

"Families?" said Katie. "None. This is my room and that's my bed."

"A whole bed to thyself?"

"You don't have your own bed?"

"Nay, I share a straw tick with three other girls and the children. How dost thou stay warm at night with only thyself?"

"I've got covers," said Katie, not sure she could actually explain how their heating system worked.

Sitting on Katie's bed, Humility stroked the quilt. "Such small and even stitches," she marveled. "I would not think such a mannish girl as thee would be such a fine sewer."

"Katie didn't make that," said Josh, walking into the room. "Mom bought it for her at the mall." Josh showed Humility a pile of magazines full of pictures of modern life, but then he had to explain the very idea of a photograph to her before she could understand what she was looking at. Josh brought in his digital camera to show her.

"Just by pressing a finger on that machine thou canst paint such a picture?"

"Yup, just like that," said Josh, and he snapped one of Humility and showed it to her. Humility played with the camera until Mrs. Lexington called them down to dinner.

Mr. Lexington had made a big lasagna. "Sit down, everyone, and say thank you to your ol' Dad 'cause I set the table tonight. Figured you and our new friend needed some time to get acquainted."

Josh and Katie immediately grabbed a seat, but Humility just stood behind a chair with her head bowed. "Go on, sweetie, take a seat," said Mrs. Lexington. "I'm afraid we're not very formal in this house."

Humility looked at her with amazement. "May I sit in this chair, then?"

"It's as good as any." Mr. Lexington smiled at her.

"'Tis so grand," said Humility softly. "I have never sat at meal before."

Mr. Lexington looked surprised. "I tell you," he said. "You find out something new every day. I would have thought for sure they had chairs in Holland. So how does that feel, Humility? Comfortable?"

Humility nodded her head. Then she reached out with her bare hand and grabbed a piece of lasagna, dripping with cheese and sauce, directly from the pan and started eating it. Red sauce was dripping all over her fingers and the tablecloth, but Humility didn't seem to notice. Mr. and Mrs. Lexington stared at her in stunned silence. She was just about to grab another piece when Josh gave a loud cough. "Here, let me serve you some," he said, taking a spoon and plopping some more on her plate.

"Mmm, this is good," said Katie, loudly. "I'm so glad I can use a *fork* to eat it." She gave Humility a small kick under the table. Humility watched her carefully and then picked up her fork, holding it awkwardly. Eventually, she managed to spear a

28

piece of lasagna, and with the sauce dripping everywhere, she brought it to her mouth. She ate it hungrily and, when there was no more on her plate, looked at the pan longingly.

"Would you like some more, dear?" asked Mrs. Lexington.

"'Tis a strange and lovely dish," answered Humility.

"It's lasagna. An Italian dish," explained Mr. Lexington a little too loudly and slowly, as if Humility didn't speak English. "I know all about those wooden shoes, but what do you Holland folks eat, anyway?"

"Besides fowl and fruits of the sea, sir, we have had much corn this harvest."

"Ah, corn," said Mr. Lexington, knowingly. "You know that's originally an American food. Introduced to the Europeans by the Indians."

"Aye. Tisquantum, the Pawtuxet, did show us how to plant the corn kernels with fish."

At this moment, Josh spilled his milk, and Katie immediately started yelling loudly at him about what an idiot he was. Mrs. Lexington rushed off to get a sponge, and Mr. Lexington urged Katie to sit down and be quiet. Amid all the hubbub, Katie whispered to Josh, "Good save!"

All during the rest of the meal, Mr. and Mrs. Lexington tried to talk with Humility. Unless they asked her a question directly, however, she kept her eyes on her plate and ate quietly. But she did seem hungry. She had three whole servings of lasagna, after Mrs. Lexington assured her repeatedly that there was enough. She ate salad. She took a piece of bread every time Mrs. Lexington passed her the basket. She drank a glass of milk, and another and another. "They must have so many cows," she murmured to herself at one point. Luckily, only Katie heard her.

"Shy kid, but she really packs it away," commented Mr. Lexington to his wife when they were loading the dishwasher after dinner.

"Practically starving," said Mrs. Lexington. "Poor thing. I feel like she's been through some dreadful trauma. Oh, I do hope we can get this all straightened out before Thanksgiving. We better hear from that Mr. Dee tonight. I wonder what the girl's poor family is thinking."

Humility had tried to help clean up, but Mr. and Mrs. Lexington had insisted she enjoy herself. Humility stood around, confused. "Hast thou wool for me to spin? Or butter to churn? I would not sit idle."

"Do you like to knit?" asked Mrs. Lexington. "I think Katie has some needles and yarn somewhere."

Katie found them, and while she and Josh rushed through homework, Humility sat at the table, the knitting needles clicking back and forth in her lap. At one point, Mrs. Lexington brought over a plate of cookies and tried to draw her out.

"Tell me about your family, dear," she asked.

Josh and Katie exchanged alarmed looks. The first few days with any Time Flyer were always nerve-racking. What would Humility say? What would she let slip? Josh and Katie had to be ready at any moment to mount a cover-up.

"My parents are dead," answered Humility

without any emotion in her voice. "And my aunt and uncle, too. But for God, I am alone on this earth."

"I knew something terrible had happened. I could just feel it!" Mrs. Lexington patted Humility's hand. She had tears in her eyes. "What happened, darling? Can you talk about it?"

"My parents died of the fevers in Holland," explained Humility, never missing a stitch with her knitting. "The dampness in the Low Lands was too hard for them. And my aunt and uncle, with whom I came over on the boat, did not make it through last winter."

"You came over on a boat?" said Mr. Lexington, coming back to the table to grab a cookie. "I didn't know anyone could afford to do that these days."

"I've heard there can be some terrible illnesses on those cruise ships," commented Mrs. Lexington, shaking her head.

"Aye, Goody Lexington. 'Twas something dreadful. All the heaving and tossing. Our mast broke and we thought for sure we were lost to the deep. But nothing was worse than that wet, cold winter in the harbor. We lost more than half our number."

"That's it for me," said Mr. Lexington. "If we ever do save up enough money to go to Europe, I'm gonna fly."

"Mom, have you heard from Mr. Dee yet?" asked Katie.

"I don't know. Let me check the computer."

Mrs. Lexington went up to her office, but in just a few minutes she was back downstairs holding an e-mail she had printed out. She pulled Mr. Lexington into the kitchen for a hushed, private conversation, but Josh and Katie tried to listen.

"I don't see why she can't return now," they heard their father say.

"I don't either, actually," their mother answered. "It's something about the time zones."

"How long does Humility have to stay here?" asked Katie, barging into the kitchen.

Their mother gave her one of her forced smiles. "No one seems to really know, sweetheart. Mr. Dee wrote that it could be a while, whatever that means."

"Goody Lexington, here are some new socks for you," announced Humility, walking in and handing her a pair she had just made.

"My goodness, those are beautiful!" said Mrs. Lexington. "Look at these, Katie. You're going to be an inspiration to us, Humility. I don't think Katie's finished so much as a scarf."

"I could if I wanted to," mumbled Katie under her breath.

Later, when Katie went upstairs to get ready for bed, she saw Humility kneeling by the footboard. "Join me, sister Kate," Humility said without looking up. "We shall confess our sins to God together and mayhap He shall deliver us from this strange confusion of times."

"Don't worry," said Katie. "I'm saying a prayer that Mr. Dee figures out how to get you home." And to herself she added, *And I hope it's soon*. She threw herself down on the air mattress her dad had put in her room earlier, and even though she thought she'd never get comfortable, she was asleep in moments. It had been a really long day.

4 A PINCH OF SALT

Katie woke up the next morning to the sound of clanging and banging downstairs. The sky was just growing light outside, but Humility wasn't in her bed.

Katie stumbled out of her room, rubbing the sleep from her eyes, and found her parents pulling on their bathrobes in the hall, looking concerned. Josh was still snoring, though.

Katie followed her parents down the stairs, with Mr. Lexington bravely going first. As they turned the corner into the living room, they instantly discovered the source of the noise. There by the fireplace was Humility, surrounded by pots and pans. When she heard them, she looked up, brushed off her skirt, and curtsied.

"What are you doing, dear?" Mrs. Lexington asked.

"I have started the fire in the hearth, mistress, and while I could not find your bucket, I have used pans to haul water from the stream."

"Stream?" said Katie. "The closest stream is near Hillside Avenue. That's four blocks away."

"I beg thy pardon, but I could not find the well. Nor could I find your cow or goat to milk. Forgive me for being idle by the fire, mistress. Now that you have all awoken, I will take out the bedding to air."

None of the Lexingtons knew what to say. Katie couldn't imagine getting up before dawn, and her parents couldn't believe a kid had actually offered to do chores, especially unnecessary ones, without being asked.

"I need a cup of coffee," said Mr. Lexington finally. "I've got a bit of a headache."

"Goodman Lexington?"

"Yes, Humility."

"I am sure there are leeches in the stream. I can return to get some for you if you want. It is often helpful to draw off the bad blood when one does have a pain in the head."

"Leeches?" Mrs. Lexington looked horrified.

"I've heard about that, Betsy," said Mr. Lexington, rubbing his eyes. "Some doctors are using them again these days."

"But not for headaches," said Katie. "I'm going back to bed. Are you coming, Humility?"

"Nay, sister Kate. 'Tis almost morning and much needs to be done for your good parents."

"Seems like Humility's going to set a good example for you and Josh, Katie," said Mr. Lexington.

"What?" said Katie, indignant. "You want me to go get you some polluted stream water to make your coffee with? Yuck!" She stomped upstairs to get dressed.

Humility went into the kitchen with Mrs. Lexington and watched her bustle about. She was amazed at the dishwasher, the electric oven, the microwave, the refrigerator, and the toaster. Mrs.

Lexington beamed with pride. "I really like to have the newest appliances. They make all the difference, don't you think?"

"How quickly they can do everything," marveled Humility.

"But somehow there's always more to do!" Mrs. Lexington sighed.

"Goody Lexington," said Humility. "I promise thee I will be no trouble and do all I can to make myself useful."

"Of course you will, dear. You've already been a big help. Look." She pointed at her feet. "I'm wearing the socks you knitted for me!"

Humility returned her smile. "Shall I sweep the house, Goody? Where dost thou keep the broom?"

"Oh, don't worry about that, sweetheart. I'll give it a quick vacuum before I leave for the office. Now you go up and get ready with Katie." She looked at Humility's long skirts and apron. "You might want to wear something . . . um, a little more American to school today. All right?"

Katie had laid out jeans, a long-sleeved shirt,

socks, and underwear on the bed. Luckily, it looked like she and Humility were just about the same size. Although Humility, underneath all of her petticoats, was probably a lot skinnier than she seemed. But when she showed the outfit to Humility, Humility refused to put it on. "Wear breeches like a man? 'Twould be immodest. Have you no laws against it?"

Katie looked at Humility's long skirt and laced vest. "Look, there are fashion laws against what you've got on. No way are you wearing that to school."

Reluctantly, Humility picked up the clothes and headed to the bathroom. A few minutes later, she emerged, looking like any modern kid. She took a big breath, looked at Katie, and pulled off her head kerchief. Her long brown hair tumbled to her waist.

"Wow! You look great," said Josh, who had just woken up and was emerging from his room.

Humility blushed. "How much easier it is to move with breeches." She walked up and down the hall, first slowly and then with more and more confidence, kicking her legs out in front of her. Her eyes sparkled.

On the way to school with Mrs. Lexington, Humility pressed her face against the car window, awed at the speed with which the world was passing them by. "'Tis like riding in the boat at full gale!"

"Sorry," apologized Mrs. Lexington. "Abner is always telling me I drive too fast on this road. But I want to get to school so we can get everything straightened out. I don't have any of your papers this time. Mr. Dee wrote that I shouldn't worry about it, but I'm not quite sure how we're going to manage getting you enrolled."

She didn't need to worry.

The office was filled with parents signing in late children when they arrived at Alice R. Quigley Middle School, but Mrs. Muhler, the principal's secretary, immediately rushed up to them when she saw the Lexingtons come in. She already knew about Humility. "We got an e-mail from the Time Flyers program this morning," she said, smiling.

"And everyone is so excited. Mrs. Lexington, these foreign guests of yours are really enriching the children's learning experience this year. We've been talking all morning about how thrilled we are to have another one."

She bustled about, producing all kinds of forms for Mrs. Lexington to sign, while all the office ladies introduced themselves to Humility. She started to curtsy, but Katie grabbed her arm and kept her standing straight.

Just at that moment, Katie noticed a mother and daughter dressed exactly alike in brown pants, silk scarves, and orange cashmere sweaters, standing in the doorway. *Oh, no,* thought Katie. *Why did we have to run into the Markles this morning? That's just what we need.*

Lizzie Markle was the most popular girl in the sixth grade — and the most dangerous. She was always making trouble for the Lexingtons, especially since their Time Flyers had started getting more attention than she did.

"Oh, my," said Mrs. Markle, looking at

Humility, her plucked eyebrows raised. "I see everyone's fussing over another one of your little guests, Betsy."

"Hello, Victoria," said Mrs. Lexington. "Yes, we've another visitor this month. This is Humility Cooper from Holland."

"Holland!" gushed Mrs. Muhler, the secretary. "I've heard such wonderful things about those tulips. Aren't we lucky the Lexingtons have brought you to us!"

Lizzie Markle snorted.

"Betsy, darling," Mrs. Markle said smoothly to Mrs. Lexington, "I think you really need to tell me more about this program. I'd love for my little Lizzie to host an exchange student."

"I can tell you all about it, Victoria, but it's awfully exclusive."

"Really?" said Mrs. Markle. "Why, how exclusive can it be if your family . . ."

She was interrupted by Mr. Walsh, the principal, coming into the office. "Welcome! Welcome!" he boomed. "It's a great day for our school when another one of the Lexingtons' Time Flyers arrives!"

"Time Flyers? Is that the name of the program?" asked Mrs. Markle, pulling a little notebook from her purse. "I'm going to have to look into that."

5 OUT OF THE FRYING PAN . . .

When Katie and Humility walked into Mrs. Chandler's fifth-grade class, the kids were all busy working on bubbling and fizzing science experiments.

"You're here at last!" Mrs. Chandler yelled over the noise of a small explosion. "I'm so excited we have another exchange student. We so enjoyed our last visitor."

"Howdy!" a boy with a badly shaved mohawk said to Humility. He held out a hand covered in green slime.

Humility stared at him, obviously horrified, and did not take his hand. "Is he one of the native peoples?" she whispered to Katie.

"Nah, it's just Brian Bucar. Humility, meet Brian." She whispered to Humility, "The hair's a long story. It has to do with our last Time Flyer, this kid from Egypt. I'll explain it sometime."

"Your hair is so long!" exclaimed Kelly Havens. "Have you ever cut it?"

"Nay," said Humility. "In my country we do not believe in women appearing as men."

"And what country is that?" asked Mrs. Chandler.

Katie quickly smiled. "Humility's from Holland, Mrs. Chandler. She just arrived yesterday."

"How thrilling!" beamed Mrs. Chandler. "We'll actually be talking a little bit about some travelers from Holland today!"

"You mean the Pilgrims?" asked Katie, a little too sharply. "Are we going to be learning about them?"

"Oh, something much more exciting than that. I have a big surprise for this class."

Great, thought Katie, who had had enough surprises in the past day.

At that moment, a beaker broke at a table across the room. While Mrs. Chandler helped clean it up, Humility looked around at the computers lined up against the wall, the tables of students pouring out steaming solutions into test tubes, the terrariums filled with lizards, the enormous plants, and the beanbag chairs in the reading corner. Her hands clenched into fists and her eyes narrowed.

"Are you okay?" Katie asked, pulling her aside.

"Are they playing at witchcraft?" Humility asked. "What is this place?"

"It's science class. I guess you don't have that at your school."

"I do not know. I have never been to school."

"You haven't been to school?" asked Mrs. Chandler, who had just rejoined the girls.

"Nay, mistress," said Humility. "But my aunt

did teach me to write my name. And I can read passages from scripture."

"Ah, I see. You've been homeschooled. That explains it. Don't worry about a thing, dear. I've worked with a lot of homeschoolers, and they are often ahead of the regular students."

But Humility struggled through the morning lessons. During silent reading time, she slowly sounded out each word in the book she'd chosen. During math, she sat in a kind of stunned silence while the other kids called out answers to a word problem on the board.

"Those children ought to be whipped for behaving so rudely to their elders," she commented to Katie on their way to lunch.

"For participating in class? How silly is that?" said Katie. She looked around the cafeteria and saw her friends Kelly and Marissa at a table together. She didn't dare sit with them, though. The last thing she needed was them asking Humility a ton of prying questions. Instead, she saw Josh and Neil playing War across the room and led Humility toward them.

"Isn't Mrs. Chandler the best?" Josh said to Humility, sliding over on the bench to make room for her. "I had her last year, and she's a lot better than the Pit Bull." Josh pointed toward his teacher, Mrs. Pitney, a squat, frowning woman with a gray helmet of hair, standing by the doorway.

"Does she let you waste your time in idleness playing cards?" responded Humility.

"Mrs. Pitney's always saying stuff like that," said Josh. He put down an ace and took Neil's ten of spades.

"Yeah. She even took our decks one day and locked them in her desk," added Neil. "By the way, I'm Neil. Josh was just telling me all about you."

"What was he telling you?" said Katie, suddenly suspicious of what Josh had given away about Humility.

"Oh, just about how . . . nice and . . . um . . . pretty . . ." stuttered Neil before Josh glared at him.

Humility blushed, and Josh coughed nervously, keeping his eyes on his sandwich.

Katie didn't know what to say. That was the last thing she'd expected.

When they all went out for recess, Katie tried to get Humility to play kickball with the rest of the girls. But she wouldn't. "Are those children really allowed to play with a ball?" she asked. "How can this be? My people would never approve of these selfish amusements."

"A lot's happened in four hundred years, Humility. Things change," explained Katie.

When the kids returned to their classroom, they found all their chairs in a circle and an old white-haired man talking to Mrs. Chandler. "Children, children, take a seat," she said. "Our surprise visitor has arrived with a very exciting opportunity for our class. Let me introduce Dr. Walker, a professor from the history department of Middlestock Community College."

She clapped her hands with great enthusiasm. The class, still red-cheeked and out of breath from recess, joined her for a second or two. Dr. Walker took a seat in one of the chairs and waited for them all to settle down.

"So," he said, when they were at last quiet, "what do you know about the holiday of Thanksgiving?"

Immediately Katie looked over at Humility. "Don't say a word," she mouthed. "That's an order. Nothing about corn or leeches or Plymouth or anything."

Humility just gave her a wide-eyed stare while kids began calling out answers.

"You eat too much turkey!" said Susie Arthur.

"Pumpkin pie and cranberry sauce!" added Mike Bettincourt.

"It's about the Pilgrims and the Native Americans," said Kelly Havens.

"They all nearly died and the Indians brought them food," said Larry Naccarato.

"My dad always watches football!" said Brian Bucar.

"Hands, please. Hands, please," begged Mrs. Chandler. A slew of hands flew up into the air, but Dr. Walker didn't call on anyone. He waited patiently for silence.

Finally, he said, "Yes, that's what we all know about Thanksgiving, isn't it? But *how* do you know it? And do you know if it is accurate information?" He peered at the students from behind thick eyeglasses.

Nobody seemed to understand his question. The hands that had been straining into the air quickly dropped. Dr. Walker let the silence grow as kids squirmed in their seats.

"This November, Middlestock Community College is hosting a history fair for all the middle schools in the county," he said. "The assignment? To investigate the first Thanksgiving. What really happened on that historic day? And how can you prove it? The team that can answer those questions most thoroughly and present their discoveries most creatively will win first prize."

"*And* a trip to Plymouth," added Mrs. Chandler. "Don't forget to tell them that."

"Thank you, Mrs. Chandler," said Dr. Walker.

"In addition to a gold-plated cup for their school, the winning team will also receive an all-expense-paid trip to Plimouth Plantation in Massachusetts."

"Cool," said Susie.

"I want to go!" said Kelly.

"Field trip! Field trip! Field trip!" chanted Brian and Larry together.

We're in, thought Katie, looking over at Humility, her hands neatly folded in her lap. *We've got the secret weapon.*

6 ... INTO THE FIRE

Katie couldn't wait to get Humility home, shut the door to her room, and start quizzing her on exactly what had happened at that first Thanksgiving. "Now you can tell me all about the turkeys you caught and how you picked cranberries, but only when we're alone, okay?" she whispered to Humility on the bus ride home. But even as the kids were walking up to the door, a frazzled Mrs. Lexington was out in the driveway urging them to get in the car.

"I've got so much shopping to do for the holiday and an appointment to show a house this afternoon and another this evening. So you all have to come with me to help. And no complaining, Josh Lexington. Off we go."

Once they arrived at the Super Shop and Save, Mrs. Lexington pulled out a crumpled list, tore it in three pieces, and handed one to Josh and one to Katie. "Josh, you head off to the frozen food section and get the vegetables and the pies. Pumpkin and apple. I may actually find a moment to make some from scratch this year, but I want the frozen ones just in case."

"I beg thy pardon, Goody Lexington."

"Yes, Humility?" Mrs. Lexington put her purse in an enormous metal cart.

"I can make pies for thee. I have made them oft for my aunt. And if you have lard and prunes, I shall make one that is most tasty."

"Oh. Well, okay," said Mrs. Lexington. "Put that on your list, Josh. Lard and prunes."

"Lard and prunes?" said Katie to herself. "*Yuck!*"

"Help me find them, Humility. C'mon," said Josh. "You push the cart and I'll scavenge." Katie watched the two of them head down an aisle, shaking her head. Something was up. It was not like her brother to want to do anything with a girl. Not at all.

When Josh led Humility into the produce section, Humility stood in a kind of trance in front of a bin of apples. "From whence has all this fruit come?" she asked Josh. "I have seen no orchards, no fields under cultivation. I have not seen even a kitchen garden near any of the houses. How can there be such bounty?"

"I guess they fly it all in from somewhere," answered Josh. "I don't really know."

In the frozen foods aisle, Josh searched for pies while Humility marveled at the packaged meals. "Whole suppers already made and no need to tend them by the fire all day long. 'Tis wondrous strange. How easy 'twould be to prepare for the Sabbath."

Suddenly, a shrill voice behind them said, "Why, it's our new exchange student!" Josh turned to see Lizzie Markle and her well-manicured mother coming up the aisle.

"My, my." Mrs. Markle peered into Josh's cart. "Buying frozen pies, I see."

"My mother always has our dinner catered," explained Lizzie to Josh.

"So tell me, young lady," Mrs. Markle said to Humility. "How exactly did you get involved with this mysterious student exchange program?"

"'Twas an accident, mistress. An accident." Humility looked to Josh for help.

"An accident? How interesting. Do explain."

"Sorry, Mrs. Markle," interrupted Josh, taking Humility by the arm. "We can't right now. My mom's in a terrible hurry. We've got to go."

Josh and Humility found Katie in the dairy section and together they dodged up and down the aisles, trying to get everything on their lists without running into the Markles again.

"You didn't tell her anything, did you?" asked Katie.

"Of course not," said Josh. "But she was really snooping."

They caught up with their mother at the checkout line, but Mrs. Markle and Lizzie were already in line right behind her. Lizzie was reading one of the tabloid newspapers about aliens and celebrities while her mother questioned Mrs. Lexington.

"Betsy," she said. "I've been doing some investigating on the Internet. That Time Flyers Student Exchange Program is an awfully strange little operation. No phone number. No address. Everything done by e-mail. It's all so irregular. Don't they want you to contact them?"

"It's very up-to-date, Victoria, very modern," said Mrs. Lexington. "These days, you can do everything on the Web, even grocery shop." She went back to reviewing her grocery list. "C'mon, kids," she said to Josh and Katie. "Start helping me unload these carts."

"But how exactly did *your* family get accepted?" persisted Mrs. Markle.

"We just filled out the form online, Victoria. That's all you have to do. And they accept you or they don't." She handed her credit card to the checkout girl.

Mrs. Markle raised her eyebrows at Lizzie.

"Careful, Mom," said Lizzie. "Your botox."

Mrs. Markle anxiously touched her forehead.

Lizzie put the magazine back on the rack and turned to Katie while her mother unloaded groceries. "Is your class doing the history fair this year?" she asked her.

"Yeah, " said Katie. "We just found out about it today."

"Well, you should just give up now," smirked Lizzie. "My cousin, Misti Markle, goes to Lakeview Middle School and her class always wins. Every year."

"Is that so?" said Katie. "She just might be in for a big surprise. Humility here is a bit of an expert on the Pilgrims."

But later that night when she was finally alone with Humility, a notebook open on her lap ready to record the facts, Katie discovered that she might not be as big a help as Katie had first thought.

"What do you mean you've never heard of Thanksgiving?" she said.

"I know not this feast day of which you speak. When first we did reach land, our men did go ashore and then we held a day of prayer and fasting in thanks to God for bringing us safely across the ocean. But no Wampanoags or Narragansett were there, although our Master Bradford did see signs of their homes and crops. Nor would we ever eat on such a day. 'Twould not be right or fit to indulge our bodies when we should be devoting ourselves to prayer and thoughts of our Maker."

"No. That doesn't sound right," said Katie. "You had turkey and pumpkin pie and cranberry sauce."

"Cranberries?"

"Yeah. Little red berries that are, like, totally sour and gross and you make a kind of jelly out of them that nobody ever eats."

Humility just shook her head. "Red berries? Perhaps thou speak of alkermes. They are red and sour and grow in the swamps. But thou art correct; we do not eat them."

Katie was about to ask more questions when there was a knock at the bedroom door. It was Josh.

"Hi, Humility," he said shyly. "I . . . um . . . made you this pencil box for . . . you know, your pencils and stuff." He held out a small, misshapen pine box with a crooked lid.

"I thank thee, brother Joshua. 'Tis a fine gift." She smiled at him, and Josh looked down at the floor. "But what is this strange bird thou hast carved on the top?"

"Oh! That's a turkey. You know, 'cause you're a Pilgrim and all."

"Some Pilgrim." Katie sighed. "She's never even heard of Thanksgiving, Josh. Humility, are you sure you sailed over on the *Mayflower* and landed on Plymouth Rock?"

"We sailed on that boat, yes. But we landed on the beach and waded ashore."

Katie threw the notebook across the room. "What a bust!"

"Is there any chance that our textbooks and teachers are wrong?" asked Josh.

"What do you mean?" said Katie.

"I mean, maybe they got it all wrong. It happened a long time ago, didn't it? Nobody filmed it or anything. And we're probably the first people ever to talk to an eyewitness."

"But an eyewitness to what?"

"To what *really* happened in Plymouth, Massachusetts."

7 SPILLING THE BEANS

All the next week, Humility was up before dawn organizing the house. She swept cobwebs out of corners, dusted bookshelves, and scoured pans until they shone like new.

"Really, dear," said Mrs. Lexington. "This is supposed to be a sort of vacation for you. I feel terrible that you're working so hard."

"Yeah, could you give it a rest?" grumbled Katie. Lately her parents had been saying things to her like, "You could take a lesson from Humility and help out around the house a little more."

One morning, Katie came downstairs and found Josh already up and helping Humility unload the dishwasher while Mrs. Lexington made breakfast.

"What are you doing?" asked Katie, horrified.

"Just giving Humility a hand. She's going to show me how to chop wood this afternoon."

"Give me a break!" Katie groaned as she threw herself onto the couch in the living room and flipped on the television. In a few moments, Humility was standing beside her, frowning.

"Dear sister Katie, I must speak to you about these vain entertainments. I am sure they are not good for your character, and as I love you, please, I beg of you, resist these temptations."

"That's right, Katie," added Mrs. Lexington. "No television before school. Isn't that the rule around here?"

Katie stormed upstairs and slammed her bedroom door behind her.

At school later that day, Mrs. Chandler gave the kids some class time to work on the history project. She'd ransacked the library for books about the Pilgrims and the early colonies for everyone to look at and was letting them take turns researching on the computer, too. But instead of working, Brian and Larry were playing computer games, and Marissa and Kelly were busy drawing pictures of fashion models. The research reading was too difficult for Humility and she ended up spending most of the time looking at pictures in the Thanksgiving books. "But this is not what Governor Bradford looks like. Not at all."

"Okay. Okay. But what about this guy? Do you recognize him?" Katie held up a drawing of a Wampanoag she'd just found.

"He is one of the natives who people the New World. What of it?"

"He's more than just a native, Humility. He's a person. And your people are gonna steal all his land and destroy his culture. It's a fact."

"Nay!" said Humility. "Our leaders have been nothing but fair in their dealings with the native peoples."

"Yeah, for now," mumbled Katie. "Anyway, didn't one of the Native Americans show you guys how to plant corn?"

"Ah, yes, yes," said Humility. "You mean Tisquantum. He can speak English because he was enslaved in Spain."

"Now we're getting somewhere," Katie said. She handed Humility the book she had been reading. It was open to a drawing that showed a long table with Pilgrims in black hats and silver buckles sitting around it. A few Native Americans sat with them. There was a roast turkey in the center of the table. "Does anything in this picture look familiar?"

Humility studied it for a long time. "The knife that man is holding. Our men carry knives like that."

"The *knife*? That's it? What about the buckles and the hats and . . . and . . . the people?"

"Nay," said Humility. "That long table and all those chairs are not ours. And those black clothes are not what our men and women wear. Nor would the Wampanoags have been robed as such."

"But didn't you ever sit down and celebrate the good harvest and all that? Didn't you get together with the Indians and make this big meal and say thank you? C'mon, you must have."

Mrs. Chandler came over to their table. "Girls, you need to stop talking and get back to work. I don't know how I can get you children to start focusing on this project."

"Mrs. Chandler," asked Katie, "is it possible that the Pilgrims didn't ever celebrate Thanksgiving? Could we have gotten it wrong?"

Mrs. Chandler threw up her hands in frustration. "Haven't any of you been doing any research?" She clapped her hands. "Pull up your chairs, class. Right now. And take out your notebooks."

"Whoa," whispered Brian to Larry. "Look at the expression on her face. She really wants to win this thing."

"All right," Mrs. Chandler said once they were all settled. "Looks like we need some background information here about the Pilgrims."

"Mrs. Chandler, excuse me," interrupted Melissa Weinstein. "But I found out in this one book that they didn't call themselves Pilgrims.

They called themselves Separatists. 'Cause they wanted to separate from the Church of England."

"Really?" asked Mrs. Chandler, surprised.

"Yeah," said Kelly Havens. "I saw that, too. Only later on, like a hundred years later, people started calling them Pilgrims."

"So what do we write down?" asked Brian. "Separatists or Pilgrims?"

"I guess Separatists, Brian," said Mrs. Chandler with a sigh. She straightened herself up in her chair. "Okay. Let's go on. So, these Separatists come to America and after an incredibly difficult trip on which many of them died before they landed in Plymouth, Massachusetts . . ."

"That's all wrong," blurted out Marissa Dwight. "Only one guy died on the trip over. A sailor."

"I read that, too," added Tali Mackenzie. "It was during the winter that everyone got sick. When they were already here. They were really cold and had run out of food, and they were living on this leaky boat 'cause they didn't have enough houses built yet."

"'Twas truly terrible," said Humility softly,

wiping a tear from her cheek. "To be so far from all that you know. To not hear the church bells in the morn, but the cries of strange animals and wild peoples in the dark and endless woods. To not know if the hardtack would last nor if 'twould be enough food in our bellies for the next day. To watch those you love feverish and failing, all around you the cries of the dying."

"Wow," said Larry. "You made me feel like I was there."

"I thought you could barely read," Kelly said to her. "Where did you find that out?"

"We've been doing some extra research at home," jumped in Katie. "Right, Humility? Right?" Katie nudged Humility in the arm.

"If you're finished, girls, I'll go on with *my* story," said Mrs. Chandler. "So, you can see the Pilgrims . . ."

"Separatists!" called out four or five different kids.

"You can see that the Separatists had a lot to be thankful for that first fall. With the help of the local Native Americans, they managed to get ashore, build homes, and plant and harvest their first crops. And their Native American friends came with turkeys and corn to celebrate that first Thanksgiving. That's the story, Katie."

"Ah, now I do see it!" blurted out Humility. "I know of this event of which you speak."

"Really?" said Katie, stunned. "You mean it did happen?"

"Of course it did," said Mrs. Chandler. "People all over the world know the story of our first Thanksgiving — and know it's true, Katie Lexington."

"But 'twas not exactly as you describe," said Humility.

"What do you mean?" asked Brian. "Did Mrs. Chandler get it wrong again?"

"Goodwife Chandler, I mean no disrespect, but 'twas not exactly as you have said."

Katie looked around the room. The whole class was staring at them. She elbowed Humility, but Humility was too caught up in her story to notice. She went on talking.

"Last month, our harvest being gotten in, four

of our men did go fowling. When the women did prepare these ducks and geese, there were enough for our whole company. The men did sport then and exercise their arms."

"Exercise their arms?" said Melissa. "What do you mean, they lifted weights?"

"Nay, they did shoot their muskets. Upon hearing them, the vast tribe of Wampanoags came with their king Massassoit — oh, more than a hundred — and so vastly did they outnumber our small company that they did kill five deer for the men to eat."

"What do you mean 'the men'?" asked Kelly. "Where were the women?"

"Cooking and serving the food, of course."

"During the whole meal?" asked Tali, fascinated.

"For the three days that the Indians were amongst us feasting."

"Us?" repeated Tali. "What do you mean 'us'?"

"What's going on?" said Melissa. "How do you even know this? It doesn't say anything like that in any of the books I've read. You talk like you were there or something."

"Yeah, what did you do?" snickered Mike Bettincourt. "Hop in a time machine or something?"

By now, Katie was in a state of panic. "Humility and I were going to surprise you," she said, interrupting the conversation. "We've been doing a lot of research on our own . . . at, um, home, and we've been talking about how we might act it out and everything. You know, for the project."

"It seems like you've been letting your imaginations run a little wild, girls," interjected Mrs. Chandler. "Not that I don't encourage this kind of creative involvement with learning, but just because you think something happened doesn't mean that it did. In order for it to be history, you need to have proof. You need to be able to show that it's true."

"But it *is* true!" cried Humility.

"Of course it is," said Katie, who knew that Humility would never have told a lie. "And we can prove it," she announced to the class. "We'll bring in the evidence from home tomorrow." But where were they going to find proof that Humility was right? She wasn't sure, but she knew they had to find it . . . fast.

8 TOO MANY COOKS

"What are you making, Mom?" asked Josh when he arrived home from school with Katie and Humility. The kitchen counters were covered in bowls, mixing cups, and cutting boards.

"I'm trying a new cranberry relish recipe," she answered. "Here, have a bite." She held out a spoon to Josh.

"Not me!" said Josh, leaving the room. "Cranberries are nasty."

"It needs more sugar. A lot more sugar," commented Katie, after trying some.

"What do you think, Humility?" asked Mrs. Lexington. She scooped out a fresh spoonful for her.

Very seriously, Humility took the spoon from her and tasted a tiny bit of the relish. Her eyes brightened and she put the whole spoon in her mouth. "'Tis most lovely, Goody Lexington. Thou art a fine cook."

"You don't think it needs more sugar?"

"Nay, 'tis so sweet already. I see that with sugar it is possible to eat alkermes."

"Alkermes?"

"I think that's what Humility calls cranberries, Mom. You know, in her language."

Humility peered into the other bowls. "What else hast thou put into this recipe?"

"Oh, just a little orange peel and some mint," said Mrs. Lexington, clearly thrilled to talk about her cooking. "Then I just mix it all up in the food processor. Of course, it will get better after it's been in the fridge a couple of days."

"Ah . . . the food processor," said Humility, looking longingly at the electric machine. "That is the one invention I would bring back with me if I could."

"You mean they're not available in Holland, dear? How surprising!"

"Mom," Katie butted in. "Humility and I have got a lot of research to do. Can we go in your office and use your computer?"

"Absolutely, kids. But no computer games. Okay?"

"Your mother is very sensible about these distractions," said Humility to Katie on the way up the stairs. "I believe her to be a good woman."

"Well, of course she is," said Katie. "She's my mom."

Up in Mrs. Lexington's office, Katie switched on the computer. While she waited for it to boot up, she tried to think of ways she could prove that what Humility said in class was true. There weren't any tape recorders or photos or movies or newscasts from four hundred years ago. What was there?

"Did anyone do any drawings or paintings the day of your harvest festival?" she asked Humility. "Try to remember, all right?"

"'Tis not hard to remember. 'Twas just last month."

"Or four hundred years ago, however you look at it," mumbled Katie.

"But nay, no one did draw. Who would waste paper for such as that?"

"What about letters home?"

"But it takes so long for them to cross the ocean. And there have been but few boats."

"This is so frustrating!" Katie said, throwing up her hands. "Here I have a real, live Pilgrim sitting beside me and we can't make use of a single thing you know because we can't prove any of it."

The moment Katie saw the tears in Humility's eyes, she realized she'd gone too far. For a long time, neither girl spoke. Finally, Humility broke the silence.

"I did not choose to come here," she began haltingly, her eyes downcast. "Nor did I even choose to go to the New World. But I have tried to accept what challenges have been placed before me."

Katie looked at Humility and for the first time wondered what it had been like not only to cross the ocean on a leaky boat into an unknown wilderness but then to be hurtled through time into a totally strange culture. "I'm sorry," said Katie. "For everything. I didn't mean to lose my temper. Mom and Dad love having you here. And Josh. I mean, I've never seen Josh like this." Katie stopped and took a breath. "And I like having you here, too."

Humility's eyes met hers. "Okay, sister Kate. Okay." She smiled as she said the unfamiliar word.

"All right, then," said Katie. "Let's get back to business. We'll figure this thing out. I know we will."

She typed the word *pilgrims* into the search engine, but when she got back almost two million sites, she decided to narrow things down. To *pilgrims* she added *first thanksgiving*. And that was all it took. Because the very first site she went to from that list had everything they needed. Just like that.

"Look at this!" Katie exclaimed. "There *was* a letter. From this guy Edward Winslow. But he wrote it in December. And that's in the future for you. I mean when you go back to the past." She shook her head. Sometimes all this time travel stuff could be pretty confusing.

Humility looked over Katie's shoulder at the computer screen where a letter was typed out. "*Our corn did prove well, and God be praised, we had a good increase of Indian corn. . . .*" she read haltingly. "'Tis true all that Goodman Winslow writes. He has always had a fair and honest hand. 'Twas all exactly as he describes."

Katie leaned back in her chair, stunned. It was so easy. The evidence was right there. The five deer killed, the ninety Indians, the shooting games. And no mention of turkey or Thanksgiving. None at all.

"I really am sorry, Humility." Katie smiled at her. "You were right. And the truth about it is totally easy to find. That's the strange thing. I wonder how come nobody bothers to find out this stuff? That's the real mystery."

"If we do bring this letter to class tomorrow, wilt our teacher believe us?"

"Yup," said Katie. "Let me just check something." She quickly visited a few more sites, including an official one from the Plimoth Plantation Museum. "It's amazing," she said. "They all say the same thing. Thanksgiving was, like, this holiday invented in the 1800s based on this one harvest festival you guys had. The turkey and cranberry sauce is a big pile of baloney. I'm going to print all this out right now."

The next morning, Katie heard Humility getting up as usual at the crack of dawn. But instead of rolling over and pulling the covers over her head, she dragged herself out of bed. *At least I could unload the dishwasher before school,* she thought to herself as she pulled on her jeans. By the time she got downstairs, however, Humility was nowhere to be seen. Katie poured herself some orange juice, opened the dishwasher, and sleepily began putting away the silverware.

When she slammed the dishwasher door shut, she sat down at the kitchen table. *I need some more sleep,* she thought, but just as she was about to head back upstairs to bed, she heard voices out on the front steps. Peeking out the front window, she caught sight of Humility with a broom in her hand. She also saw the shadow of someone else. "Who's that?" she wondered. And then she got a better look. It was Lizzie and Mrs. Markle, in matching fluorescent pink jogging suits, talking to Humility. That was all it took for Katie to instantly wake up.

"So you're not even really an exchange student, then?" Mrs. Markle was saying to Humility as Katie yanked open the front door. "Why, hello, Katherine," she said. "I've just been having a nice little chat with Humility here. Your mother certainly is getting a lot of use out of her."

"My name is Katie, not Katherine. And what are you two doing here, anyway?"

"Mom and I were out for our morning power walk when we saw poor little Humility here lugging these big heavy trash cans out to the street."

Lizzie Markle patted Humility on the arm, giving her a sympathetic look.

"Humility likes to do chores, don't you, Humility?" said Katie.

"Aye, sister Kate," she answered. "I was just explaining to Goody Markle that I try in many ways to show your family gratitude for giving me room and board when I was so unexpectedly thrust upon them."

"Yes," said Mrs. Markle. "And you came to this country with other members of your religious cult? Is that correct?"

"Religious cult? What have you guys been talking about?" snapped Katie.

"All kinds of stuff!" said Lizzie, excitedly. "How she came over on this crowded boat with all these other people and how they went up and down the coast looking for a place to land and a lot of them died and . . ."

"It's a very interesting exchange program your family is participating in, Katherine. Very interesting indeed." With her manicured hand Mrs.

Markle took the broom from Humility. "Dear, why don't you put that down? A young girl like you should really be getting your beauty rest."

Katie grabbed the broom away from Mrs. Markle and handed it back to Humility. "Look, Mrs. Markle. Humility can do whatever she wants. Okay? And if you want to know anything about Time Flyers, you can visit their Web site, just like my mom told you to."

Mrs. Markle smiled at Katie. "But I *have* visited that Web site. I certainly have. Only now I'm beginning to understand why the program is so secretive. Come, Lizzie, let's get in another mile before you have to get ready for school." She looked at Humility and shook her head. "Don't despair, dear. Help is on the way. We'll find a way to get you home to your people."

Katie was fuming. "My parents will do that, Mrs. Markle. This is none of your business."

"By the way, *Katherine*," said Lizzie, pausing as she descended the steps, "I was at my cousin

Misti's last night, and her whole class was at her house sewing authentic woolen costumes for the history fair. What is *your* class making? Construction paper Pilgrim hats?" Lizzie giggled and skipped off after her mother.

9 MADE FROM SCRATCH

"What do you mean we can't make pumpkin pie?" said Kelly Havens in class later that week as all the kids worked on the history fair project.

"The Separatists didn't eat it," said Katie. "They didn't have any sugar left that fall, or many spices or ground flour for a crust. You can make squash mush if you want."

"I have a recipe for squash mush right here," said Marissa, who'd just been on the computer.

All week long, Katie had been collecting information from Humility about what the Pilgrims had actually eaten and worn and done at that first harvest meal in 1621. As soon as she had the information, she got on the Internet and hunted for some backup material to share with the class. Now other kids were hot on the trail for real evidence, too.

"I'm so proud of you all for using primary sources." Mrs. Chandler beamed when they produced copies of old letters and diary entries.

"You have no idea," mumbled Katie.

"Hey, guess what I just found out," said Brian. "Did you know those dudes ate swans, Mrs. Chandler?"

"Swans? No way!" said Larry.

"Really?" Katie whispered to Humility.

Humility nodded her head and whispered back, "They are most tasty."

"You girls are going to be doing a lot of cooking and sewing for this thing," said Brian, leaning back in his chair. "Remember, the women did all the cooking."

"Ah, then, Brian," said Humility, giving him a sly grin, "thou shouldst leave to go hunting today with thy friends and bring back fish and fowl for us to eat. And hast thou tended the fields and harvested the corn? And built new houses for the winter fast approaching?"

"All right, Millie, I get your point. I'll make some mush," conceded Brian. "But I want to be an Indian when we do the actual presentation."

"Thou hast the right style of hair, certainly," she said, smiling at him again. "But where, I have wondered, are the real native peoples of this land? Since I have arrived, I have seen none. Are their encampments so far off?"

"You mean you thought when you came to America you'd see some real Indians?" said Larry. "What? Like in a western?" He laughed and started bouncing up and down in his chair like he was riding a horse.

"Settle down, Larry," said Mrs. Chandler, laying a hand on his shoulder.

"I'm part Native American, Mrs. Chandler," said Marissa, popping up. "My grandmother was part Cherokee."

"Way cool, way cool," said Brian. "You can

be an Indian with me for the project!" They high-fived each other.

All this time, Humility was looking from one kid to another, a puzzled expression on her face.

With the project due to the community college the next Monday, everyone decided they would meet on Saturday at the Lexingtons' house to have Humility help them make authentic clothing. "She's a sewing whiz," explained Katie, and Humility perked up slightly at the compliment. But for the rest of the day, while the class discussed how they'd get all the food and costumes made, Humility seemed distracted. Only after the bus had dropped them off at home did Humility share her thoughts with Josh and Katie.

"So the Indians are all gone," she said thoughtfully.

"Not all gone," said Katie. "I've never met one, but they have reservations and stuff you can go to. I mean, there are still some around."

"Some," repeated Humility. "But there were so many. Why did they all leave?"

"It wasn't exactly their choice," answered Josh,

carefully. "How much are we allowed to tell her?" he asked Katie.

Katie stopped. "I don't know. She's found out plenty already about the future — about inventions and history and all kinds of stuff. What's one more thing?" Katie let her heavy backpack slide off her shoulder and looked directly at Humility. "It's bad news, Humility. The Native Americans were almost wiped out. They got all kinds of horrible diseases like smallpox from the Europeans, and their lands were stolen, and they were massacred. Finally, they were driven farther and farther west until they had almost nothing left. And then we said that we discovered America. I'm sorry."

"But *we* did not do this!" protested Humility, horrified. "We didst pay them for all their land, and we live peacefully with the Wampanoags. There are but fifty of us and scores upon scores of tribes. Whole nations of tribes. What cruel nonsense do you speak?"

Josh lay a gentle hand on Humility's arm. "She's

not lying, Humility. Your people were probably pretty nice and all, but more people came, and more people, and then more people after that."

Humility's eyes brimmed with tears. "What you say is too terrible. Is there nothing we can do for them?"

"We can make sure they're remembered at the history fair next Monday," Katie said.

Humility nodded. "We will make sure of it."

That Saturday, the kids met at the Lexingtons. They brought bolts of fabric, old Halloween costumes, frayed woolen blankets, and whatever else they thought they could use to create authentic seventeenth-century clothes.

"Doesn't everything have to be in gray and black?" asked Kelly. But Katie, after a hurried conversation with Humility, explained that the Separatists wore all kinds of different colors.

"We're gonna win this thing. C'mon, Plimouth Plantation! Here we come!" said Brian, trying unsuccessfully to thread a needle.

Humility was amazed to discover that only a

few of the kids knew how to sew. "I know that you do buy your garb at shops, but how do you mend them?" she asked.

"Mend them?" said Larry.

"You just buy new ones. Who wants to wear some old funky, messed-up clothes anyway?" said Marissa.

"Such waste." Humility sighed.

The work went slowly, with lots of pricked fingers. Mrs. Lexington had tried to get them to use her sewing machine, but all the kids had decided that wouldn't be authentic. By the end of the day, they had completed only a few costumes. They managed to turn an old pair of leather pants into Wampanoag leggings for Brian and an old wool blanket into a Separatist dress for Kelly.

"This stuff is so itchy," said Kelly, modeling it for everyone. "How did they stand it?"

"Thou thinkst that is itchy." Humility laughed. "Thou must try it with lice and fleas and the salt water clinging to thy skin day after day."

"No, thank you," said Kelly. "I don't want to be *that* real."

"Shall I order up some pizzas?" asked Mr. Lexington, coming into the living room.

"A splendid idea, Goodman Lexington!" said Humility. Since her introduction to lasagna that first night, Humility had become an enthusiastic fan of Italian food.

When the pizzas arrived, all the kids crowded around the table and only a few managed to get chairs. The rest stood around grabbing slices from the cardboard boxes. "Now, this be authentic!" giggled Humility to Katie. "Everyone standing around and all hands in the same pot." She bit into a huge slice of pepperoni.

Just as they were digging in, the phone rang. "It's for you, Katie," Mrs. Lexington said.

Katie took the receiver and went into the kitchen where it was quieter. "Hello?"

"Hello, *Katherine*."

"I'm busy, Lizzie," said Katie. "We're working over here."

"I know," she said. "It's just too bad it's all going to be for nothing."

"What do you mean?" Katie said sharply. She heard something in Lizzie's voice that scared her.

"Only that my mother and I have figured out what you're up to."

"What we're up to is getting our project ready. What's the big deal?"

"Oh, I'm not talking about the project. I'm talking about something much, much bigger than that. Have fun on Monday. 'Bye, *Katherine.*" With a click, Lizzie hung up.

"What was all that about?" Josh asked Katie.

"I don't know. But Lizzie's up to no good again. I'm just worried she's figured out something about Time Flyers."

"Don't you worry," said Josh. "I'll keep an eye out for you on Monday at the history fair."

"You're coming with us?" said Katie, surprised. "Why? Your class isn't involved."

Josh blushed. "It's a big moment for you and Humility. . . . I mean . . ."

"Yeah, I get it," said Katie. "You don't have to say anything else."

She headed back into the dining room, where everyone was laughing and finishing up their pizza. "All right," she announced. "I think we better work out a schedule for tomorrow. It won't be hard to get all the cooking done, but we're going to have to work like demons to finish these costumes."

"Everyone's welcome to come here again," said Mr. Lexington. "My fifth-grade class once put on a production of *Georgie, Get Your Musket*. One of the best times I ever had. Why, I remember . . ."

"Great, Dad. Later, okay?" interrupted Katie. "Can everybody come tomorrow?" One girl had to go to her grandmother's, but everybody else started nodding their heads and shouting "Yeah!" and "What time?" Everybody, that is, except for Humility.

Her voice was soft but firm, and as soon as she started speaking, all the other kids stopped chatting. "I am afraid we can do no work tomorrow. We must accept what we have accomplished and take the day for rest." She folded her hands, looking very serious.

"What are you talking about, Mill?" said Brian. "Tomorrow's Sunday. We've got the whole day to get stuff done — even if we sleep in."

"Yeah," said a bunch of the kids. "What's the big problem?"

Humility waited patiently for them to settle down and then spoke again. "Tomorrow is the Sabbath and we will do no work."

"But, Humility," said Katie, "all you've been doing since you came here is work. Now the one day we actually need you to do something, you're checking out? I don't get it."

"Tomorrow is the Sabbath," Humility insisted. "I have been surprised at the ways of thy people since I have come here. Lazy and slack about chores all week. Then, when it dost come time to rest and devote thyselves to God, so busy running about to entertain thyselves. 'Tis all wrong."

"Is it against your religion to do *anything* on Sundays?" asked Kelly.

"We do go to meeting and listen to scripture," said Humility.

Everyone just stared at each other.

"We go to church," said a couple of kids. "But that doesn't mean we can't get together and sew some costumes and glue some displays."

"I didn't know the Dutch were so religious," commented Mr. Lexington to his wife, who'd been listening. "That's the thing about these Time Flyer kids, Betsy. I'm learning something new every single day."

Katie jumped in. "If you don't want to help us, Humility, that's okay. We'll get it done ourselves." She turned her back to Humility and was just about to start reorganizing the class when Humility interrupted her again.

"Nay, sister Kate, I will not let thee nor thy good parents work. Not tomorrow."

"Wow," said Larry. "You are so deep."

"If Millie says it, we gotta do it," said Brian.

"She's the man." He gave her a big smile and stretched back in his chair.

"We can meet at my house," said Kelly, ignoring him.

"But none of us knows how to sew." Marissa moaned. "Humility's been showing us how to do *everything*!"

Katie shook her head. "What a waste. Now we're gonna lose for sure."

10 THE ICING ON THE CAKE

On the bus ride over to the community college on Monday morning, Katie took a good look at their group. Kids had done the best they could to piece together and finish their costumes, but some had on T-shirts with their beaded leather skirts, or blue jeans tucked into long white soccer socks. Still most of the kids were dressed as Wampanoags instead of Separatists. *Oh, well,* thought Katie. *At least we've got really good displays documenting our sources and a lot of food.*

Most of the kids held some kind of steaming pot. There were seafood dishes with clams and mussels, a duck someone's mother had roasted, and even some venison one kid, whose dad was a hunter, had been able to bring.

"I don't mind if the judges eat this stuff," said Larry. "I just hope we don't have to."

"What didst thou make? Squash?" Humility asked Brian.

"Nah. I hate vegetables. My mom and I made *frumi*-something with corn."

"Furmenty! How good of thee! I must needs try it." She smiled at him.

You know, thought Katie. *She's a bit of a flirt. I never noticed it before, but she really is.*

As they clambered off the bus, Katie looked for her mother, who was driving over with Josh. But the parking lot was crowded with school buses and with kids in all kinds of costumes. Marissa pointed out one group who had pumpkin pies in their hands and black construction paper hats on their heads. Not a single one of them was dressed as a Native American. "At least we've beat that group," she said to Katie.

"But what about them?" said Katie, pointing. Striding up the walkway ahead of them was an orderly class of kids in wool and leather.

"Wow!" said Kelly. "Look at those costumes. Every single one looks just like Marissa's and Brian's."

"And no pumpkin pie, you can bet on it." Katie sighed. "Look. There's Misti Markle. I heard that group was good."

"Who are those dudes?" said Brian. He pointed to four men standing by the entranceway to the college, in dark suits and sunglasses.

"Whoa!" said Larry. "Those guys look tough."

"I sure hope they're not the judges," added Kelly. "We're done for."

Inside the hall, kids were busy setting up displays and preparing themselves to be interviewed by the judges. The kids from Alice R. Quigley Middle School were right beside Misti Markle's class.

A very blond girl, dressed in an outfit that looked as if it had time-traveled with Humility, sauntered over to their table. "Hi. You must be Katherine Lexington," she said to Katie. "My cousin has told me *all* about you!" She giggled and went back to her group.

Just at that moment Mrs. Lexington arrived with Josh in tow. "Dear, I'm sorry we're late," she began breathlessly. "We've had a very difficult morning. I've left your father at home to deal with Immigration."

"Immigration?" said Katie, confused.

Behind their mother, Josh frantically waved his arms, indicating to Katie that he needed to talk to her in private.

"I don't know, Katie. This is really, really, really bad," said Josh once the two of them were alone in a corner of the room. "These guys just swarmed all over the house this morning after you left, demanding to see Humility's passport, and now they're accusing Mom and Dad of harboring illegal aliens. Something crazy about how they're smuggling foreigners in by boat to be servants for people. But Dad managed to get them all quieted down by showing them the Time Flyers Web site. He explained how Humility was with you at the history fair and that, of course, she has a passport. So I ran upstairs while they were talking and I started looking through Humility's stuff. . . ."

"Wait a minute. *You went in my room?*" demanded Katie. "You aren't allowed in my room!"

"I *had* to, sis. What else was I going to do? What if they deport Humility? Where would they send her, anyway? Or what if they arrested Mom and Dad? Or worse yet, what if they found out all about Time Flyers and then they started subjecting us to all these weird experiments and stuff? And then I bet we'd never get our turn to go back in time. And you know Humility doesn't have any passport. Anyway, I felt like I had to check just in case she has some kind of official identification. And while I'm looking through her stuff, I notice the hourglass. I pick it up and what do you know? The sand is pouring through it. What are we gonna do?" He showed her the hourglass. The golden sand was now streaming from one end to the other.

Katie was just taking it from him when she noticed her mother talking to the men in sunglasses she'd seen earlier. Mrs. Lexington's purse was open and she seemed to be showing them her driver's license.

"Oh, no!" said Josh. "More of 'em. Those look just like the guys who showed up at the house earlier. We've got to go help Mom out."

"You go," said Katie. "I can't. The judges have just arrived at our table. Our class is getting interviewed right now!" They rushed off in different directions.

Josh reached his mother just as she was explaining to the men that she'd dashed off an e-mail to Mr. Dee, the director of the program, that morning and she was sure he could sort everything out for them.

"Ma'am, we're gonna need a phone number and an address for this program, not just some hastily put-together Web site."

"It's a foreign program," interrupted Josh, hoping to distract the men. "*Real* foreign."

Meanwhile, Katie arrived at her table to find the kids apologizing to the judges for their unfinished costumes.

"We knew exactly what they were supposed to look like," said Kelly. "But Humility here wouldn't let us do any work on them yesterday."

"Yeah, 'cause it was the Sabbath or something," said Larry.

"Interesting. Very interesting," said a woman in a tweed suit and horn-rimmed glasses. A balding man was tasting Brian's furmenty. He spit it out into a napkin.

"No sugar or spices in this furmenty, young man," he said.

"Nah. You gotta remember those dudes didn't have much left of that stuff from England and Holland. Sugar, spices — that stuff was all gone."

"Indeed it was, young man. Indeed it was."

Brian gave the thumbs-up to Humility.

While the other kids finished answering the

judges' questions, Katie pulled Humility behind one of the displays. "Do you have a passport?" she asked.

"Of what dost thou speak?"

"Yeah, I didn't think so. Whatever you do, don't talk to those men in those suits over there, okay?" Humility looked over at them and nodded. "And here, hold this," added Katie, handing Humility the hourglass. "I don't know what's going on, but Josh noticed the sand was moving. Once it's gone . . . well, so are you — *if* you're holding it."

"Thou meanest I will return to Plymouth?"

"I think so. And soon."

"I will be sad to say farewell to thee, sister Kate." Humility hung the hourglass around her neck.

Katie looked at Humility. "I will miss you, Humility. I kind of like having a sister. Even if she does do more chores than me . . ." Both girls laughed together.

Josh rushed over to them. "It's amazing," he said. "They were totally insistent about seeing

Humility's passport and then, one of them gets this phone call and, the next thing you know, he says to the others, 'We're letting this one go.' Just like that. And the other one says, 'Why, chief?' and he answers, 'Word's come down from higher up. This one's untouchable.' So, for some reason, we're okay."

"Josh, I think Humility's going to be disappearing really soon."

"Oh, man! This is awful!" said Josh. "Humility, I just want you to know that if there's any way — any way at all — I'm coming back to visit you in Plymouth."

"And if there is not," said Humility, "know that I will find some way to leave there a sign that I remember thee both." She touched Josh's arm. He turned as red as Humility's cloak.

Loud cheers suddenly filled the hall, and Katie, Josh, and Humility peeked out from behind the display to see Mrs. Chandler holding an enormous gold-plated trophy. All three judges were standing beside her. "While the fifth-grade students from

Alice R. Quigley Middle School may not have been as completely dressed as some of their peers," the tweedy woman was saying, "nevertheless their garb showed an awareness of both authentic seventeenth-century clothing and Wampanoag wear."

"Most impressive, however, and what distinguished this group from all others, and why they have been awarded first prize," continued the bald man, "was their understanding of the Separatist mind-set. They did not just do excellent research, sew real costumes, and make authentic dishes. No, they *became* Separatists, and rather than labor on Sunday, like our famous forebears, they forswore all work to observe the Sabbath."

The fifth-graders looked from one to another, completely astonished.

"Humility rules!" exclaimed Brian.

"You go, girl!" shouted Larry.

"Humility rules! Humility rules!" yelled all the other kids in Mrs. Chandler's class.

Later, some kids said they had heard a sonic

boom behind the roar of cheering. Others said they had seen a flash of blue light. But Katie and Josh saw Humility cheering with all the other children, and then, just like that, disappear into thin air.

EPILOGUE: LEFTOVERS

When Mrs. Chandler's class got back from their field trip to Plimouth Plantation, Katie showed her photos to Josh, while their parents were busy putting the last touches on Thanksgiving dinner. Soon Josh and Katie's cousins would be arriving from upstate. Their mother was basting the turkey, their father was mashing potatoes, and a pumpkin pie was cooling on the shelf. Beside it was a prune tart, which Katie had made herself that morning in honor of Humility.

"This is what the boat was like that they sailed on," she said, holding up a picture of the replica of the *Mayflower* that they had visited. "And these are what their houses looked like," she continued, handing him a photo of a thatched-roof cottage from the historical reenactment village. There were people in the picture dressed up just like Humility had been when she first arrived. "Those are people who pretend to be real Pilgrims. They were pretty good," Katie added.

"Cool," said Josh. "But it must have been kind of a letdown after having met a real Separatist."

"I guess," said Katie, watching Josh carefully as he thumbed through the photos.

"What's this?" said Josh pulling out a dark, close-up photo of a piece of wood.

"Oh," said Katie, suppressing a smile. "I'm not quite sure. You know the houses in the park are just copies of the real ones. But we visited one place that actually was from the seventeenth century, a real house from those times. And I was just leaning against the wall listening to our guide when I saw this carved into one of the beams. Take a good look."

When he looked carefully, Josh could see carved

into the old, darkened wood some kind of symbol. Two triangles were arranged on top of each other, the points of each just barely touching.

"What is it?" said Josh. He held the picture upside down and then right side up.

"Don't those two triangles together look like an hourglass?"

"An hourglass? Really?" said Josh. "It could be anything. There's no way of knowing if Humility carved it."

Katie nodded her head. "Keep looking."

Just barely visible, almost rubbed away by time, were four letters. *HC* at the top of one triangle. *JL* at the bottom of the other.

"*HC? JL?*" Josh looked confused. "What does that mean?"

Katie grinned. "I wonder . . ."

And at that moment, Josh turned bright red.

BACK WITH HUMILITY IN PLYMOUTH COLONY, 1621

Some time in early October, just after you bring in the first crops, your governor sends four men out "fowling," hunting migrating ducks and geese. The men are so successful that they celebrate with some shooting practice when they return. The great Wampanoag king, Massassoit, brings ninety men to join you. They kill five deer and prepare for three days of feasting. At this celebration are mostly Native Americans — not Europeans. After a brutal winter with little food and much disease, there are only fifty-two of the original passengers from the *Mayflower* left alive.

You don't think of this as Thanksgiving. For

you, a Separatist, a day of giving thanks to God involves prayer, scripture reading, and fasting. Fasting means you don't eat anything at all, and certainly not turkey and pie.

What you are actually celebrating with all your hunting and cooking and eating on that lovely day in October is a harvest festival like the ones your ancestors have celebrated for hundreds of years back in England.

A month after this feast, Edward Winslow will write a letter home which will include a brief description of those three days. That will be the only record of what will become, three hundred years later, a very different holiday.

Why You Came to America

Your family left England for Holland in 1608 because you wanted to separate from the Church of England. Unlike the Puritans, who wanted a

stricter, "purer" form of
worship, your people, the
Separatists, don't want
anything at all to do with
the state religion of
England. Unfortunately,
that's against the law,
so you all sneak away
to Holland. In Holland, people have religious
freedom and are allowed to worship as they
please.

Because you are not Dutch, however, it's hard
for your family to make a living in Leiden, Holland,
where you live. Plus, your parents worry that you
are going to stop speaking English and marry
someone Dutch. Twelve years later, it's time to
separate again. Your family books passage to
America on the *Mayflower* and hopes you will
find a better life in the New World.

Pilgrims?

In a sermon ten years after you arrive in the
New World, one of your preachers will refer to

you all as pilgrims. That's *pilgrims* with a small *p*. By *pilgrims* he just means that you are travelers on a spiritual journey. Until the 1800s, *all*

of the early American settlers will be referred to as pilgrims. Only when Abe Lincoln makes Thanksgiving a holiday during the Civil War will your people become known as Pilgrims with a capital *P*.

The New World

You arrive in Cape Cod in 1620 and then sail on to Plymouth, where there is a better harbor. You probably didn't land on Plymouth Rock. Maybe one or two of you did. Until more than 140 years later, no one paid any attention to that big hunk of granite on the shore. The only evidence you landed there? A ninety-four-year-old man in 1741 says that his father, who arrived on a different boat in 1623, told him that he had been told by one of the original settlers that they'd landed on this particular rock. None of the original *Mayflower* travelers, however, mention the rock in any of their descrip-

tions of the first landings at Plymouth. So who knows?

The First Year

Getting to America is hard, but surviving there is even harder. While only one person (William Butten) dies on the trip across, more than half of the passengers and half of the crew die of disease that first winter. Most of your food is gone or rotten by the time you complete the crossing, and there's no time to plant crops when you arrive before the winter. You manage only to get a couple of houses built before the snows start. Most of you have to live on that cold, leaky, wooden boat all winter long.

What You Ate

That first year, you survive on food from the ocean — the bay is teeming with fish and eels, lobsters crawl along the sea floor, and it's easy to find mussels and clams by digging at the beach. In the spring, your Native American friend Tisquantum (known today as Squanto) and the Wampanoags show you how to plant corn and where to find local food — grapes, plums, salad greens, and herbs. That part is absolutely true!

You don't eat pumpkin pie. You can't make a pie crust. You don't have a mill to grind flour yet, you don't have any sugar left, and you have only a little butter. But you do eat all kinds of squashes and pumpkins stewed into mush. Delicious!

As to cranberries? Try one. *Sour*! It'll be fifty years before any Englishman mentions boiling this berry with sugar to make a sauce. When you arrive, you think they are alkermes — a berry you know from Europe.

Squash Mush (WITH TWENTY-FIRST-CENTURY MEASUREMENTS)
4 cups boiled, steamed, or baked squash
3 tablespoons butter (if you have it)
2 to 3 teaspoons cider vinegar
1 or 2 teaspoons ground ginger
1/2 teaspoon salt
Mash the squash. Then, in a saucepan over medium heat, stir and heat all the ingredients together. Adjust seasonings to taste (but don't add sugar), and serve hot. Yum!

Sitting Down to Dinner
Oops! You don't. Not unless you're the head of the household — he gets the chair. That's right — *the* chair. The rest of you stand around the table and reach your hands into the communal bowls. Your only eating utensil is a knife and

maybe a clamshell you use as a spoon. Forks have just been invented in Italy, but only really rich people are using them so far.

"This is finger lickin' good!"

The Sabbath

It's your only official holiday. You don't celebrate Christmas, Easter, or any other traditional religious feasts, but you keep the Lord's Day every week. You get ready the day before — cooking, cleaning, and finishing chores — so that on Sunday all you have to do is read the Bible and pray. When you first landed in the New World after three long months at sea and had just begun to explore Cape Cod, you stopped everything on the Sabbath and stayed on the boat. You wouldn't budge, much to the dismay of the crew. You take the Sabbath very seriously. Oh, and anyone who breaks it? Watch out for the stocks! The stocks are a wooden frame that holds your wrists or your ankles. You're stuck in it in the middle of town, and everyone can come and make fun of you and throw rotten food or mud — or worse — at you.

You and the Wampanoags

Plymouth Colony is actually the site of a Patuxet village. All the Patuxet people died during an epidemic a few years before you arrive. The only remaining Patuxet is Squanto, known as Tisquantum to his own people. He survived because he was kidnapped years earlier by English fishermen and sold as a slave to Spanish monks. Eventually, he worked his way back home only to find it settled by the Europeans he'd just escaped from.

He helps you plant corn and develop a working relationship with the Wampanoag tribe and their chief leader, Massassoit. After years of disease and fighting with the Narragansett Indians, Massassoit is eager for a powerful ally. The Wampanaogs and the Separatists will enjoy one of the longest periods of peace between Europeans and the native peoples — almost fifty years.

You are not a tolerant people, however.

(Remember all that separating?) Nor are your neighbors, the Puritans, who settle the Massachusetts Bay Colony. They don't even allow different kinds of Christians — Quakers or Baptists — to live with them, much less people who don't share any of their religious beliefs. Eventually, more and more Europeans will arrive and fight the different tribes for their land. You will also bring with you new diseases that are devastating to the native peoples.

In 1600, there were probably as many as 12,000 Wampanoag people living in forty different villages. By 1700, there will be fewer than 400 left alive. But the Wampanoag will not disappear. In the twenty-first century, the tribe will claim a membership of about 3,000 people, many still living near modern-day Plymouth.

The Real Humility Cooper

Governor William Bradford, in his book of memories about the Separatists, *Of Plimoth Plantation*, writes that "Edward Tilley and his wife both died soon after their arrival, and the girl

Humility, their cousin, was sent for into England and died there." That's all that's known about her. A Humility Cooper was baptized in London in 1638 at the age of nineteen. If this is the same girl, she was only a baby when she arrived in Plymouth. But again, there's no way of being absolutely sure they are talking about the same person. No one knows anything else about her . . . except Josh and Katie Lexington!

ABOUT THE AUTHOR

Perdita Finn grew up twenty minutes from Plimouth Plantation and spent many a cold November field trip imagining what it would be like to live there. She now lives in the Catskills with her husband, two children, four cats, and a dachshund who likes pumpkin pie.